Withdrawn

DON'T FEED THE GECKOS!

CHRONICLES ··

—— BOOK THREE ——

DON'T FEED THE GECKOS!

BY Karen English

ILLUSTRATED BY
Laura Freeman

Clarion Books
Houghton Mifflin Harcourt · Boston · New York

For Gavin and Jacob and all their friends.
— K.E.

For my mom, who was stronger and braver
than she believed she was.
— L.F.

Clarion Books
3 Park Avenue
New York, New York 10016

Text copyright © 2015 by Karen English
Illustrations copyright © 2015 by Laura Freeman

Clarion Books is an imprint of Houghton Mifflin Harcourt Publishing Company.

www.hmhco.com

The text was set in Napoleone Slab.
The illustrations were executed digitally.

Library of Congress Cataloging-in-Publication Data
English, Karen.
Don't feed the geckos! / by Karen English ; illustrated by Laura Freeman.
pages cm. — (The Carver chronicles ; book three)
Summary: When Bernardo comes to live with Carlos temporarily,
taking over his top bunk, his spot on the school soccer team,
and even his Papi's attention, Carlos knows he is not happy, but worse,
Bernardo starts messing with Carlos's pet geckos, so Carlos tries to see past
his cousin's annoying ways and keep the peace for his family's sake.
ISBN 978-0-544-57529-5 (hardback)
[1. Cousins—Fiction. 2. Geckos—Fiction. 3. Schools—Fiction.
4. Hispanic Americans—Fiction.] I. Freeman-Hines, Laura, illustrator.
II. Title. III. Title: Do not feed the geckos!
PZ7.E7232Don 2015
[Fic]—dc23
2015013602

Manufactured in the United States of America
DOC 10 9 8 7 6 5 4 3 2 1
4500561202

• Contents •

One
Company Coming

Carlos's cousin, Bernardo, is coming. It's after school and Carlos sits down at the kitchen table to eat his Toaster Tart and eavesdrop on his mother and Tía Lupe's telephone conversation. His mother and Tía Lupe are always on the phone, checking with each other about everything. At least once or twice a day. His father doesn't even answer the phone anymore because he knows it's probably Tía Lupe.

Carlos overhears that his cousin Bernardo is coming to stay with them all the way from Texas because Bernardo's mom — Tía Emilia — is having a rough time and needs to get a fresh start somewhere else. She's moving to their town and sending Bernardo ahead.

Carlos stops chewing to listen better. Now it sounds

as if his mother and Tía Lupe are gossiping about Tía Emilia. She's always having problems; she doesn't make the right choices; she needs to manage her life better; and blah blah blah. Boring grown-up stuff. But it does make him think about his cousin and the fact that he's coming tomorrow.

His mother finally gets off the phone and comes to sit across from him. She puts on her serious face.

"Now, listen here, Carlos. Do you remember your cousin Bernardo?"

"A little bit." Bernardo was kind of chubby and had a mop of dark curly hair. Carlos went with Mami and Papi to Texas — San Antonio — when he was almost six and his sister, Issy (short for Isabella), had just turned three. It was Bernardo's birthday; Carlos turned six a few months after him. Carlos remembers sitting on a porch, eating a Creamsicle with Bernardo before his birthday party. Oh, and running through the sprinklers. He remembers Bernardo cried because he wanted two pieces of birthday cake on his plate at once. He didn't want to wait until he finished what he had first. He just sat there crying and looking stupid with a mouth full of chewed-up cake.

And Carlos remembers seeing a photograph of Bernardo's dad in some kind of uniform—like an army uniform.

"Bernardo and Tía Emilia are mov- ing here. Your *tía* wants him making the change in schools and settled as soon as possible. I'm picking him up to- morrow, so I just want to give you a heads-up."

Maybe this will be a good thing. Maybe Bernardo will be cool and it'll be awesome to have another guy in the house—kind of like a brother. They'll be able to do things together. Mami doesn't let Carlos go to the park by himself, or the store, or anywhere, actually. But with his cousin Bernardo here, he'll have an automatic buddy to go places with. *Yeah,* Carlos says to himself. *Bernardo.*

"What's he like?" Carlos asks.

"How am I supposed to know?" Mami says, sounding a little irritated. "All I know is that you better make your cousin feel at home. Make him feel welcome."

That's important to Mami, Carlos knows. Family. And sticking together and helping each other out.

Now Mami is giving him a list that she's counting out on her fingers — which shows she means business. She still has the serious face where she stares at Carlos, looking at him closely. His little sister comes into the room and stands next to Mami. She's wearing her tiara because she wants to be a queen when she grows up. It's annoying. Ever since Mami told her she was named after Queen Isabella of Spain, she's been wearing that tiara as much as possible. Mami did a report on Queen Isabella in high school, apparently.

"Can I have a Toaster Tart?" Issy asks in a whiny voice.

"Not now, Princess."

"Queen," Issy says. She adjusts her crown. Carlos rolls his eyes.

"Oh, right. *Queen* Isabella. Not now."

Issy must sense that there's something going on

that she wants to be a part of. She climbs onto Mami's lap, and then there are the two of them, looking at Carlos like they expect something special from him.

Bernardo has had a hard year, Mami tells him. She doesn't tell him what that means exactly, but because he has had this hard year, Carlos is to make Bernardo feel extra "at home." Like letting him feed Carlos's geckos. Stuff like that. "And introduce him to your friends, help him in school, share stuff with him."

That sounds super, but Carlos is stuck on letting Bernardo near his geckos. *Uh-uh . . . Ain't gonna happen.* At least not without supervision.

In the last few months, Carlos has discovered a love for animals — and insects. Different kinds of animals, like geckos and horned toads and albino snakes. He also realized he loves insects and their weird behaviors. Because of this, Carlos is no longer a member of the Knucklehead Club. He used to always miss turning in his homework, he did a sloppy job on his projects, he didn't always study for spelling tests, he brought toys to school to play with in his desk, and he didn't do his classwork in a timely fashion. Just a general knucklehead.

Those were the words of his teacher, Ms. Shelby-Ortiz, actually. He'd overheard her talking to Mr. Beaumont, the other third grade teacher, in the front office. She'd said, "I've got a few knuckleheads in my class this year. I'm hoping they'll decide to straighten up." She didn't know Carlos was listening.

He had come into the office to see if he could call his mother and tell her to bring the lunch he'd forgotten (typical knucklehead behavior), and he was standing right behind the two teachers as he waited his turn to speak to Mrs. Marker, the office lady.

He'd left after that. He didn't want Ms. Shelby-Ortiz to know he'd heard. He went back out to the yard and sat down on the nearest bench, thinking he'd just ask a couple of kids for whatever they could spare out of their own lunches.

It wasn't time to line up yet, so he'd had time to think — about being a *knucklehead*. He didn't want to be thought of like that. It made him feel funny. What if he went through his whole life being known as a knucklehead?

Besides, when he'd helped Papi fix the back door screen that Saturday, Papi had told him that if he wanted to be one of those new things he was talking about all the time — an entomologist or a zoologist — he'd have to go to college.

Could he get into college? Could he be an entomologist (a person who studies insects) or a zoologist (one who studies animals) while being a knucklehead? He didn't think so. That really bothered him.

Two
Mami Still Talking

Mami is still talking — but once Carlos stops thinking about the knucklehead life, his thoughts return to Bernardo. Bernardo messing with his geckos: Darla, Peaches, and Gizmo . . . He doesn't think so. *Uh-uh.*

Carlos frowns. Just a little, so his mother doesn't really notice. Those geckos are fragile. They have to be taken care of just so. He barely lets Issy look at them. When Richard and Gavin come over and want to take one out of the terrarium and hold it, Carlos stands over them, watching closely so they don't scare the gecko or handle it the wrong way. Sometimes he'll only let them look at his geckos.

And then there's his ant farm. He's had that ant farm for three months. A person has to be especially gentle around an ant farm. No jiggling. Even a little jiggling can collapse a tunnel. Everything is especially sensitive in an ant farm.

You have to send for the ants after you get the farm. Which he did, though some were already dead on arrival. The information that came with the farm warned against just getting ants from any ol' place. If you weren't careful, you could get ants from two different colonies. Then they would fight each other. They wouldn't be cooperative and do the teamwork thing that ants do.

He'd carefully placed the farm on a little table in the corner of his room by itself. Just to ensure it wouldn't be exposed to any kind of jostling. Now, with Bernardo coming, he'll have to sit him down and explain all of this. He thinks about that. Didn't Bernardo breathe through his mouth and walk around with a kind of blank look on his face when he saw him last? Would he be able to grasp the words of warning?

The only way he allows Issy to look at the ants is if she sits in the little chair at the table where the ant farm is and keeps her hands folded. No touching, no pointing, no even breathing too hard on it. Just *looking*.

Soon he'll have his butterfly habitat, too. Papi said he could get one if he scored a hundred percent on the next five spelling tests. He has only two more to go. Then he'll be able to see the butterflies go from a larva (or caterpillar) to a chrysalis to a butterfly.

"What do you feed those things?" Richard asked one time when he and Gavin were over to practice soccer dribbles and they were looking at the geckos.

"Crickets."

"Yuck," Richard said. "Where do you get those?"

"At the pet store."

"Do you feed them with your hand, or do you just dump the crickets in?"

"Either way, but you have to be careful," Carlos had said.

"And the crickets are alive?" Gavin asked.

"Well, yeah."

There are so many things people just don't know about geckos.

○ ○ ○

Now, even though his mother is searching his face to see if her words are sinking in, Carlos is thinking, *No way. No way am I going to let that guy touch my geckos. Or my ant farm.*

Soon Mami's back to counting on her fingers: "I want you to put fresh linens on the top bunk."

"But that's *my* bunk, Mami."

Issy is smiling at him as if she's enjoying herself. Sometimes she likes to see Carlos flustered.

"I'm thinking Bernardo will probably prefer the top bunk — so let him have it." Mami pauses. "Clear out a dresser drawer so he'll have a place to put his socks and pajamas and stuff."

Underwear, Carlos thinks. He knows his mom means underwear too but just doesn't want to freak him out.

"Let me see. What am I missing?" Mami looks up toward the ceiling.

That's enough, Carlos wants to say.

"Oh, yeah. I want you to go up and give your bathroom a good scrubbing."

Oooh. This is bad. What his mother means by a good scrubbing, no kid should ever have to do. It means scouring the sink and tub, mopping the floor, and cleaning the *toilet.* Yuck! Who does he know who has to give a bathroom a good scrubbing? No one. That's what mothers are for. Not little kids. But his mother always says, "You mess up . . . you clean up." And she always has Papi onboard. He never disagrees with her. It's like he's obeying Mami as well. Then she usually tells Carlos all the chores she had to do as a kid — and Carlos thinks, *Oh, gosh, here it comes.*

"You think we had a dishwasher? What a joke. And a clothes dryer? I had to hang the clothes on a line with clothespins. You don't even know what a clothespin is, Buddy Boy."

Mami always calls him Buddy Boy when she's making a point about her childhood. She calls him Buddy Boy and his sister Miss Priss. Anyway, he does know what a clothespin is, because sometimes Ms.

Shelby-Ortiz uses clothespins to attach their artwork to an overhead string going from one end of the classroom to the other.

"And take him out in the backyard and let him kick around your soccer ball. Show him some moves. Make him feel like he's good at something. Your *tía* Lupe says some kids at his old school weren't very nice to him."

That gets Carlos's attention. Why were some kids not nice to Bernardo? What's with him? He almost asks this, but something tells him that it would just start up a long lecture from Mami about bullying and standing up for the bullied person and being careful not to blame the victim. So he keeps that question to himself.

Mami goes on. "You make sure your friends are nice to Bernardo. And the other kids in your class, too."

Carlos bites his lip. How's he supposed to do that?

"He's coming by himself?"

"Not exactly. Your *tía* Lupe's neighbor is coming here to visit some family. So she's bringing Bernardo with her."

"How are they getting here?"

"On the bus."

"Why not on an airplane?"

"Because not everyone's rich, Doofus."

That's another word Mami uses for Carlos. She called him that a lot after the last parent-teacher conference, when his parents learned he'd been acting up a little: messing up on spelling tests, playing with toys in his desk, and talking without raising his hand and waiting to be recognized. All that seemed natural before he turned over his new leaf. In fact, he once marveled at how kids like Nikki, Gavin, and Erik Castillo managed to keep it all together. They were the three best students in Ms. Shelby-Ortiz's class. And it didn't even seem hard for them. Scoring hundreds on spelling tests and multiplication-facts quizzes was nothing to them. It was probably like breathing for those three.

But now that he was being good, or at least better — paying attention, studying for spelling tests, and no longer bringing little toys from home to play with at every sneaky opportunity — he actually felt okay about comparing himself to Nikki and Gavin and Erik. He kind of looked at people like Calvin Vickers and Ralph Buyer with pity.

"How long's he here for?"

"For a while," his mother says, and Carlos thinks, *Funny how grownups can answer a question without really answering it. Like, how long is "for a while"?* It could mean anything: a few months; a few years.

"And he's going to be in my class?"

"Right."

"How long's a while?"

"Don't you worry about that, *mi hijo*. You just worry about the things you need to worry about."

Carlos frowns. What is it he's supposed to worry about? He definitely worries about soccer — that he's not very good at it. He wants to please Papi, but he can't really say he *loves* soccer the way Papi does. Carlos likes animals and insects more. (Not more than his mother and father and Issy in her tiara, but a lot). Sometimes, Carlos worries that he will never be chosen to be office monitor. And now he's worried about the next spelling test.

Three
Bernardo

My cousin's coming," Carlos says to Richard and Gavin the next day while they sit in the cafeteria.

Richard is blowing bubbles into his carton of milk. When he finishes with that, he gulps down some air and lets out a big burp. He grins and looks around as if he's proud of his achievement.

"When's he coming?" Gavin asks.

"Today. After school."

"He's going to live with you?" Gavin asks.

"For a while."

"How long is that?"

"I don't know."

"What's he like?" Richard asks.

"I haven't seen him since I was little. He was kind of big and . . ."

"And what?" Gavin asks.

"And . . ." Carlos says again—but he can't put it into words. "It's hard to explain."

● ● ●

The bus station is crowded with travelers. Mami checks a paper in her hand and then looks up at the numbers above the doors of the idling buses. "Thirty-two . . . There it is," she says. She leads the way to a nearby bus.

People skip or slouch down the steps of the bus and then go wait by the luggage hold with their eyes peeled for their bags. Carlos watches the passengers. No Bernardo. At least no one who looks like the Bernardo he remembers.

Mami glances up at the bus's number again. "Yes. This is it." She watches the passengers as they go by, too. She checks her watch. Carlos glances down the rows between the idling buses. Then he feels a hand on his shoulder. When he turns around, there's Bernardo. Same face, but on a much bigger body. Still plump and kind of a blockhead, but half a head taller than Carlos. He's grinning widely.

"Hey, Carlos," he says. He's got a small bag of popcorn in his hand that he shoves into his canvas carry-on. Carlos thinks that Bernardo probably doesn't want to share. That's okay. Carlos wasn't in the mood for popcorn anyway.

"Hey, Bernardo," he says. Walking toward them is a woman with wire-rimmed glasses and a purple scarf around her neck, and lots of bags hooked onto both arms.

"Mrs. Ruiz?" his mother says.

The plump woman hugs Carlos's mother lightly. "This must be Carlos," she says, grinning down at him. "Boy, Bernardo's sure been talking about you."

"Really?" Mami says.

Carlos is surprised. He has only met Bernardo once — when he was five. What could Bernardo have been saying about him? They reach the parking lot, and Mrs. Ruiz sees the daughter who has come to pick her up. Mrs. Ruiz waves, hands Bernardo his luggage, and hurries to a small car. At one point, she looks back and says brightly, "He's all yours."

What's that supposed to mean? Carlos wonders. He looks over at Bernardo. He has a smug look on his face as if he's amused by some private joke.

Mami reaches down and gives Bernardo a hug. "My, what a big boy you've gotten to be," Mami says. Then she frowns as if she hopes Bernardo isn't taking that the wrong way — that he knows she was referring to height, not width. She turns to where she thinks she parked her car and leads the way, pressing the clicker thing on the key to sound the beep that will tell her where it is. Mami is always forgetting where she's parked.

Bernardo keeps grinning at Carlos and, with no warning, punches him in the arm — hard. It hurts. Carlos frowns and looks to his mother, but she's already walking briskly toward their car in the middle of a far row. He rubs his sore arm. He looks to Mami again, but she's no help. Somehow, that seems to signal the way it's going to be.

"Now, this is where you're going to sleep, Bernardo," Mami says. They're standing in the middle of Carlos's room while Mami pulls out the empty dresser drawer and shows Bernardo where he can put his clothes. She opens the closet and shoves Carlos's clothes aside on the rod. "You can put your clothes that need to be hung up in this closet, and Carlos is giving you the top bunk."

Carlos looks up at his sanctuary. That's his one spot — in the whole house. That's where he gets to play Hay Day (a video game with farm animals) without being bothered by Issy or his mother noticing and telling him to put that thing down and get a book. His top bunk is where he searches for information about weird animals or weird insects on his tablet. That's where he gets to imagine becoming either a zoologist or an entomologist when he grows up. Maybe both. That's where he gets to look down on his world and dream.

The world of his room, with the ant farm and the gecko aquarium and soon a butterfly habitat, is a reflection of him. It has *Carlos* written all over it. It contains everything he needs to relax . . . and to learn stuff that he can explain to Issy.

"A butterfly pops out of the furry worm?" she'd asked, when he was trying to explain the stages of a butterfly.

"No, there's another stage called the chrysalis stage."

"What?"

"You'll see." He didn't know how to explain the chrysalis stage.

His thoughts turn back to his future career. Maybe he can even get a Mason Bee house to hang from the maple tree in the backyard. He'll have to convince Mami about that one. He'll have to wait for the right time.

Just before Mami goes back downstairs, she turns to Carlos and says, "Go get Bernardo a towel and washcloth."

Carlos looks at Bernardo, who's standing in the

middle of the room, looking around. He hurries to the linen closet, grabs a washcloth and a towel, and when he comes back, he sees Bernardo peering into the terrarium.

"What are those?" Bernardo asks.

"Those are my geckos," Carlos says, his heart beating in his ears.

"Are they real?"

"Of course they're real."

"How come they're not moving?"

"That's what they do. They kind of look like they're posing. It's a defensive thing." He moves between the terrarium and Bernardo.

"But what's there to defend themselves from? There's just the three of them."

"It's just part of their behavior. They're programmed that way."

"What do you mean 'programmed'?"

Carlos searches for the words. It's difficult to explain.

"So what are their names?" Bernardo presses on.

"Darla is the one on the rock, Peaches is behind the

rock, and Gizmo is probably in his little cave thing."

"What kind of names are those?" Bernardo turns to Carlos.

"Well, two are females and one's male. I just came up with those names."

Bernardo makes a grunting sound. "What do they eat?"

"Crickets, mostly. We get them at the pet store."

"And that's it? Sounds kind of boring."

Bernardo starts to reach into the terrarium, but Carlos stops him. "Just leave them alone for now. I'll let you hold one later."

Bernardo looks at Carlos for a moment as if he's deciding whether to do as Carlos says. He looks back at the terrarium, and a tiny smile plays on his lips.

Then he moves to the bunk bed, climbs the ladder, and perches himself in the middle of Carlos's bed. "Hey, I like it up here."

Carlos had hoped that since Bernardo was on the big side, he wouldn't want to climb up and down the ladder. No such luck. He notices Bernardo is still wearing his shoes.

"Hey . . . You have your shoes on."

"Yeah."

"You can't sit on my bed with shoes on."

"How come?"

"Just take them off before you get on my bed."

"It's *my* bed now."

What can Carlos say to that? Thanks to Mami, it *is* his bed.

"So, Bernardo," Papi says at dinner, "you think you'll like it here?"

Bernardo takes a bite of his lime chicken. He chews and swallows. "My mom makes this with cilantro," he says to Mami. Then he turns to Papi. "It's okay. I guess I have to see. I'm going to miss my friends."

"Did you have a lot of friends in Texas?" Mami asks.

"Yeah. I had a lot of friends."

Carlos glances at Mami, to see if she believes him. But Mami's face doesn't show much.

"What else are you going to miss?"

"I'm going to miss my soccer team."

"Oh. Soccer," Mami says.

"Yeah, and they're going to miss me, too. 'Cause I score most of the goals."

"Wow," Mami says. "Now, that's interesting. We need a good soccer player for Carlos's team."

What does Mami mean by that? Carlos wonders. Just because he's had a few bad games, that doesn't mean she should count him out.

"Well . . . we're going to try real hard to make you feel at home. Right, Carlos?" Mami says, turning to him.

"Yeah," Carlos agrees.

Suddenly Bernardo is squirming in his seat. "I need to go to the bathroom," he says.

"Sure, go ahead," Mami says.

After Bernardo leaves the table, Mami turns to Carlos. "I'm going to talk to Coach Willis and see if Bernardo can be on the team. I think that will make him feel even more at home. Don't you think that's a good idea, Carlos?"

Carlos can't really think just then. He's busy listening to the sounds upstairs. Did Bernardo really need to go to the bathroom? Could he be in Carlos's room, messing with his geckos or his ant farm?

"Carlos?"

"Huh?"

"What do you think about Bernardo being on your soccer team?"

"Yeah, yeah — okay."

"What's that supposed to mean?"

Carlos is almost certain he hears steps above his head in his bedroom. "I mean, yeah, that's fine, Mami." He takes a sip of milk. "Can I go to the bathroom too?"

"Wait until Bernardo comes back."

"But I can use your bathroom."

Mami sighs. "Okay," she says. "Don't be up there all year."

Four
You Can't Feed a Gecko Popcorn!

Carlos takes the stairs two at a time. He nearly bumps into Bernardo just as he reaches the landing. Bernardo smiles and reaches back as if to give Carlos a punch. Then he drops his hand and laughs.

Carlos watches after him until he disappears down the stairs, and then ducks into his own room. He checks the ant farm. All the tunnels seem to be undisturbed. The ants are still busy doing ant things. Then he turns to the terrarium and spots several kernels of popcorn on its floor. A kernel has been placed on top of Gizmo's cave!

His breath quickens; his fists clench. He can't believe it. *Popcorn!* Luckily, the geckos have ignored the food. Probably because they can't chase it around the terrarium. Maybe they thought the popcorn was some kind of plant.

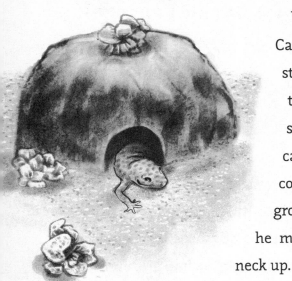

Whatever the case, Carlos storms down the stairs, marches into the dining room, and says to Bernardo, "You can't feed a gecko popcorn!" He feels his face grow warm. He knows he must be red from the neck up.

"What?" Bernardo turns to him, his eyes wide with innocence.

"Don't say you didn't put popcorn in the geckos' terrarium." Carlos waits. He can't believe Bernardo would try to lie.

Bernardo looks at Mami. Mami is looking back and forth between Carlos and Bernardo. He drops his head and raises his eyebrows forlornly. "I thought they'd like it."

"What?"

"Yeah, I was feeling kind of sorry for them, 'cause all they ever get is crickets. Crickets, crickets, crickets. I know I'd get tired if all I ever got was crickets."

"You're not a gecko! They're very special creatures. You can't just give them any ol' thing!"

Carlos looks to Mami with a helpless expression.

"Carlos, don't make such a big deal of it. No harm done," she says.

Carlos looks to his father. Papi shrugs. "They're still alive, right?"

Carlos takes a big, deep breath and lets it out slowly. He can't bring himself to speak. He hunches over his plate and resumes eating, but he's lost his appetite.

● ● ●

Later, while Mami does the dishes, Papi takes Bernardo out in the backyard so Bernardo can show him what he's got . . . soccerwise. Though Carlos is all the way up in his room studying his multiplication facts, he can hear Papi and Bernardo dribbling the soccer ball back and forth between them.

"In this dribble, remember to connect with the ball using the inside of your foot, and stay on your toes,"

Papi is saying to Bernardo. Then Carlos hears, "Good! You're a natural."

Carlos marches over to his open window and closes it. He doesn't want to hear anything positive about Bernardo just now.

Later, after homework and his shower, when Carlos goes downstairs to get ice cream and watch basketball with Papi, he hears Mami saying to Bernardo, "Yeah, the team is kind of struggling right now, and I have a feeling you'll be a great addition."

She and Papi and Bernardo are sitting in front of the basketball game, eating ice cream. Carlos doesn't get it. Is anyone going to notice that he's there? Even Issy, sitting cross-legged on the floor, doesn't look up from her coloring book. What's wrong with this family?

And what does Mami mean that the team's been struggling? He flops down into the easy chair facing the TV. He pokes out his lower lip a little bit — enough

to let everyone know that he's still annoyed about the popcorn. The problem is, no one seems to notice.

Bernardo just won't go to sleep. He hasn't bothered to take his shower yet or brush his teeth, and now he's up there on the top bunk, playing his loud video game, with his legs hanging down practically in Carlos's face. Carlos has to get to sleep. He's exhausted, and he doesn't want to be tired at school the next day.

"Are you going to take your shower and brush your teeth? I'm finished with the bathroom."

"Why should I do that?"

"You don't brush your teeth before you go to bed?"

"No. I brush 'em in the morning. If I have time."

"Oh," Carlos says. He waits a few minutes, then says, "How long you think you're going to play that video game?"

"Asphalt Eight? I don't know. I'm not sleepy, so . . ."

"But you're tired, right?"

"Not really."

Carlos closes his eyes and tries his best to go to sleep. Just when he thinks he can't stand the noise of the game any longer, Bernardo turns it off and falls back on the bed. It's quiet. Finally.

But before long, just as Carlos is drifting off, he hears snoring. Bernardo has fallen asleep, but he's snoring like a bear.

Oh, no, Carlos thinks. *This is torture.*

He has to admit that so far Bernardo is kind of a disappointment. And Carlos cannot forget that punch.

Five
First Day

As soon as they enter the schoolyard, Mami, Issy, and Bernardo go one way, to the office, and Carlos goes another, to his line. He feels relieved.

"That your cousin?" Gavin asks as Carlos slips into the line behind him. They have to wait for Ms. Shelby-Ortiz to pick them up from the yard. They're supposed to be standing like soldiers, hands to themselves, mouths zipped, facing straight ahead. Gavin, Richard, and Carlos watch Carlos's mom walk Bernardo into the school building.

"He's kinda . . . *big*," Gavin says.

"Yeah," Carlos agrees, rubbing his shoulder absently.

"What's he like?" Richard asks.

"Hard to say."

"He's going to be in *our* class?"

Carlos nods. "Uh-huh."

○ ○ ○

The first thing Carlos notices when he enters the classroom is that there's an open topic for morning journal. "Yes!" he says under his breath. He's got a lot to say. Stuff he wants to get out. He's probably the only one of the four students at Table Two who likes to write. In the past, writing was always a big groan. A struggle. But for some reason, it's getting easier and easier. He simply writes what he'd say if he was explaining out loud something that happened to him. He just has to remind himself to go over his work to see if it's okay. Ms. Shelby-Ortiz has told everyone that they should read their journal entries to themselves when they think they're finished. That's the way to catch the mistakes and to see if what they've written is clear. It will help them get rid of all those pesky run-on sentences and confusion.

Carlos takes out his pencil and begins:

My cousin Bernardo is here. At my house. He's going to stay with us a while until his mother gets here and picks him up. I don't think Bernardo has a father anymore. I want to ask him, but I think I'll wait. Mami will just tell me its not my bizness. Maybe he was in the army or something and didnt make it. Or something. I don't know if I like Bernardo. He has a funny personallity. I think hes kind of sneaky. And I don't like that he gave me a punch on the arm for nothing when I first met him. I didnt do nothing to him. Nothing. And he just punched me hard on the arm. My arm is still sore. I didn't tell because I didnt want him too get in trouble but he better not do that again just because hes bigger than me. I dont know how long he's going to be with us. Well, that all I got to say about Bernardo. Oh and hes bigger than I am and a little older than I am. Oh and he fed popcorn to my geckos. He could have made them choke. Now I'm kind of worried about my geckos. Because he's in my room and he has the top bunk. Thats not even fair.

Carlos reads over what he's written under his breath. It sounds good. He looks around. Almost everyone is still writing. He knows he should take out his Sustained Silent Reading book, but he chose the wrong one. It's really boring. He'd like to get another book, but Ms. Shelby-Ortiz says you need to give some of them a chance. Stick with them, because they can start out boring and then get good later.

Sometimes Mami will say, "Go in your room and read and don't come out for thirty minutes." Then she'll warn, "And if I catch you playing with a video game or looking up something about some animal, I'm going to have you sit at the kitchen table and read right in front of me. And I'm going to take that video game and you won't see it for a month."

Sometimes he wonders if mothers just think up stuff to make kids miserable. When she says this to him, he'll go into his room, feeling like he's being punished. He'll start reading, but before long his mind will be wandering all over the place. Just on its own. He'll think of soccer — the different ways to pass the ball—then he'll start looking at the video game on his dresser, wanting to play it so bad.

While he's reading, the video game will keep popping into his mind. Or he'll remember a pass he messed up during the last soccer game.

Mami will call out, "How you doing up there with *Sign of the Arrow*?"

And he will say, "Fine." But he won't be doing fine, because Mami got the book from the library and read

it herself, and there will be questions. Detailed questions.

She'd loved *The Sign of the Arrow* when she was little and told him, "You'll love it, too." And he'd believed her. "For one thing, it's a boy book, and it has a lot of adventure," she'd said. Yeah, he could tell by the picture on the cover of a boy hiking along some mountain trail that it was going to have adventure.

But the adventure has been slow to build up, and he keeps skipping pages, looking for the good part. He skips ahead for a few pages, goes back to where he left off, and tries to remember what happened.

Soon, he'll hear his mother call up to his room with, "Come here, Buddy Boy. I need you to summarize chapter three for me." He'll come down to the kitchen, taking his time, and sit across from her while she's got her nose in chapter three, waiting for him to summarize it. And there he'll be, trying hard to remember what happened in chapter three.

"That's what I thought," she'll eventually say. "Get back up there and read chapter three *again*," and he'll think, *Ughhh*. Why couldn't books be like video games? Fast moving. Exciting. He doesn't say that out loud, but that's what he says in his head.

● ● ●

"Who's that guy?" Carlos hears Rosario ask. She sits across from him at Table Two. He follows her gaze to see Bernardo, Ms. Shelby-Ortiz, and Mami standing together near the door. Mami has Issy by the hand. She's being extra good. Ms. Shelby-Ortiz and Mami are talking, and Bernardo looks like he's sizing up the classroom. He moves over to the jigsaw table and stares at the puzzle of extinct species, which is nearly finished.

Room Ten is proud of the one-thousand-piece jigsaw puzzle. It's the first time the class has worked on one with a thousand pieces. Ms. Shelby-Ortiz has promised that when it's all finished, she'll put that special jigsaw puzzle glue on it and then she'll hang it on the wall — by the door, so all the kids from the other classes can see it when they walk by.

"Class," Ms. Shelby-Ortiz says. She holds up one hand and puts her finger over her mouth with the other. Everyone else does the same to show that they are listening, including Carlos. Then they all put their hands down. Everyone is quiet — showing Ms. Shelby-Ortiz that they have their listening ears on.

"We have a new student." She beams to drum up enthusiasm. "We're all going to show Bernardo here what a great place Carver Elementary School is. Right?"

Some kids nod slowly. Some say, "Yes, Ms. Shelby-Ortiz." Some look at Bernardo skeptically. His T-shirt hangs out, and his hair looks a little messy. Carlos notices that, once again, he's breathing through his mouth — and when he remembers to close it, it's set in kind of a sneer. Carlos scoots down a little in his chair and looks out the window. But soon he hears his name.

"Carlos, I'm going to let you take Bernardo under your wing and show him the ropes: where the bathroom is, the cafeteria, et cetera, et cetera. He can have one of the empty cubbies for his lunch and book bag, and"—she claps her hands and looks around—"the pencil sharpener rules . . . He'll need to know those and also the rest of the class rules. In fact, Richard, switch to the empty desk across from Antonia and let Bernardo have yours."

Bernardo stands there waiting. His eyes look a little distant, as if he's bored with all this introduction stuff.

"That's your cousin?" Carlos's tablemate, Ralph, whispers to him.

Carlos nods.

"Where'd he come from?"

"Texas."

"Where the cowboys live?"

"I guess," Carlos says, imagining cowboys and horses and lassos. He sees Mami and Issy leave.

"How long is he going to be here?"

Carlos had been putting rubber markings on the top of his desk with the edge of his pink eraser. Now he begins to clean them away. He looks up at Ralph. "For a while," he says.

Ms. Shelby-Ortiz begins pulling materials and

books that Bernardo will need from the shelf near her desk. She signals for Carlos to give her a hand. She piles books into his arms, and Bernardo's arms too. There are also workbooks and a cardboard pencil box and a morning journal and spiral notebooks. All of this is carried to Bernardo's new desk right next to Carlos's.

Ms. Shelby-Ortiz comes over with a brand-new name tag for Bernardo. She removes Richard's name tag and tapes Bernardo's to the upper right-hand corner of his desk. It's as if Bernardo has even moved into Carlos's space at school. It's like they're joined at the hip, the way some identical twins are born. Carlos just can't get away from him.

Ms. Shelby-Ortiz consults her plan book. "Okay . . . We still have time to finish up our morning journals before reading. Carlos, will you explain to Bernardo what we do with our morning journals?"

Carlos pulls the fresh new journal out from the pile of books — books Bernardo has made no effort to place inside his desk — and says, "This is your morning journal. Every day after we put all our stuff away, we check the board for the topic, and then we write on that topic." Carlos points to the board. Bernardo glances toward it. His face is blank. He looks as if he didn't get enough sleep the night before. Which is strange, because Carlos is the one who didn't get enough sleep. He had to listen to Bernardo snoring almost all night long.

"See, today is open topic. That means you can write about anything you want."

Bernardo suddenly perks up. "What did you write about so far?"

"Me?"

"Yeah."

Carlos doesn't really want to say. There's some stuff that Bernardo might not find too flattering. "Oh . . . I just wrote some stuff, you know. About the weekend."

"Can I see it?"

"Uh, we don't have that much time, and some-times Ms. Shelby-Ortiz has us pass them in so she can check them over. Better get started."

Bernardo opens his brand-new morning journal. He looks over at Carlos's. Carlos has decorated his with bugs and animals. Bernardo sits there, staring.

Then he picks up his pencil and looks at the lead.

He tests its sharpness on his finger. He opens his journal to the first page.

"Put today's date in the upper right-hand corner. That's what Ms. Shelby-Ortiz tells us to do."

Bernardo looks up at the board to see the date, then proceeds to write it in the upper right-hand corner of the page. He has to look up several times to get the spelling right. Carlos can hear him breathing through his mouth. Carlos takes out his book that he's "reading for pleasure" and opens to where he left off.

A few minutes later, Ms. Shelby-Ortiz is saying, "Okay, class, pencils down. Rosario, collect the journals for me." Carlos looks over at Bernardo's open journal. There are only a few lines written in large, messy print. He's not surprised.

Six
All the Best Kickers

Recess is better, because Room Ten has the kickball and jump rope areas, and Carlos doesn't have to watch over Bernardo. He only has to point out the boys' bathroom when Bernardo needs it and send him on his way.

Carlos wants to be on Ralph's team. If Ralph played soccer, he'd be one of the best kickers on the Miller's Park soccer team. Calvin Vickers is the other team captain, and somehow Carlos knows Calvin's going to pick him.

As Room Ten's players stand in a group, waiting for Calvin to pick his first teammate, Carlos mutters quietly, "Don't pick me . . . Don't pick me."

"Carlos," Calvin Vickers says.

Carlos sighs and goes to stand behind him.

Ralph calls out, "Emilio."

Another good kicker, Carlos thinks.

Calvin calls out, "Gavin."

"Shoot," Carlos says under his breath, and watches while Gavin makes his way over and gets behind him. Gavin may be good on his skateboard, but he's only so-so at kickball.

Richard gets on Ralph's team, and that gives Ralph's team the advantage with three good players. Calvin spies Bernardo walking across the yard, returning from the boys' bathroom.

"Okay, we'll get the new guy," he says.

Carlos looks to see Bernardo lumbering across the yard to the baseball diamond they use for kickball. *Oh, no,* he thinks. *This is not good.*

Bernardo trudges up to Carlos. "What are you guys doing?"

"Choosing up sides for kickball," Carlos says. "You're on my team."

"Cool," Bernardo says. He looks confident.

Ralph and Calvin keep choosing up sides until each team has six players.

"Play ball!" Bernardo yells, and everyone turns to stare at him.

"I just like saying that," he explains, and then looks down, grinning at the ground.

● ● ●

The teams flip a coin to see which will kick first. Ralph's team wins. *More bad luck,* Carlos thinks. Ralph chooses himself to be the first kicker. No surprise there. He wants to start off the game with his team on top.

"Hey, let me pitch!" Carlos yells to Calvin, who's looking over his team. "I always get it over the base." Calvin checks him for a second, then tosses the ball to Gerald. "You pitch, Gerald."

Carlos's shoulders slump. He knows Calvin is still mad because Carlos didn't let him cheat off his paper last week during the spelling test. Carlos shrugs and finds a place near first base. Bernardo saunters to third. The other team members spread out over the field.

Gerald pitches a slow, easy roll, and Ralph kicks a high ball straight between second and third. It lands right in Bernardo's outstretched arms. "Out!" he cries.

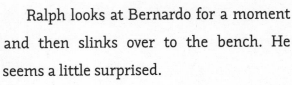

Ralph looks at Bernardo for a moment and then slinks over to the bench. He seems a little surprised.

Before Ralph sits down, he switches places with Emilio so that he can quickly have another shot at kicking. For some reason, Emilio doesn't seem to mind. The other players let this go as well. Too many squabbles can cut into play time. The next ball Gerald rolls is a bit wobbly and goes a foot to the left of home base. Carlos would have done better at pitching.

"Ball!" Ralph yells out, using a baseball term.

Gerald pitches again. The ball rolls wide of the mark once more, and Ralph doesn't even try to kick it.

"Ball two!" he yells out.

Carlos slaps his forehead. *What a team!* "Hey, Gerald! How about getting it over the base?"

Gerald whips around and bounces the ball once — hard. "You think you can do better?"

"Yeah!"

Gerald ignores him and pitches the ball fast and wild. It doesn't even go near home base.

Carlos takes in a deep breath. "Ball three!" Ralph cries. "One more and I walk!"

"Let me pitch, Calvin!"

Calvin looks Carlos up and down. "Okay." He turns toward Gerald. "You're on first!"

Gerald bounces the ball low and hard to Carlos and stomps to first base. Carlos grabs it like he doesn't even notice his fingertips are stinging, then takes his place at the pitcher's spot and rolls the ball fast — with no bounces — and catches Ralph by surprise. Ralph is all ready to call out "Ball four," but he doesn't have a chance. The ball is crossing the base, leaving him barely enough time to get into position.

His foot slips across the ball, and he nearly stumbles kicking it. It goes nowhere, but Ralph runs toward first base anyway. Erik Castillo, behind home plate, grabs the ball and throws it toward Bernardo, just as Ralph is rounding first and heading toward second base. Bernardo is right where he needs to be. He catches the ball, runs to second, and stomps on the base before Ralph can reach it.

"That's two outs!" Bernardo cries. He bounces the ball once — hard — to emphasize his point. Carlos is impressed, but not really surprised. Even though Bernardo's kind of big, that doesn't always mean a person won't be athletic. Bernardo's big — *and* a good kickball player.

That's what Carlos tells Papi in the car after school. Usually Mami picks him up, but she has a dentist appointment, and Papi has a day off from work for some reason.

Carlos goes on. "If it wasn't for Bernardo, we would have lost. Because not only was Bernardo good in the field, he was a good kicker."

"Really?" Papi says. He checks Bernardo in the rearview mirror. Bernardo's busy looking out the window, as if he has other things on his mind.

Carlos is a little disappointed. He thought pumping up Bernardo to Papi would make Bernardo act nicer later — at home. But Bernardo doesn't even seem to notice.

"Wow," Papi says, seemingly impressed.

"I'm good at all sports," Bernardo says out of the blue. Carlos feels a bit irritated.

"You can't be good at *all* sports," Papi says.

"Well, the important ones."

Carlos glances at the back of Papi's head, wondering what the expression on his face is right now. Carlos is sure that Papi will have a response to that.

"Every sport is important to the people who play them," Papi says.

"Well, I'm talking about the main sports, like baseball and football and basketball . . . and soccer. I'll probably play on Carlos's team. I think they're going to need me."

Carlos thinks maybe Bernardo's gotten his hopes up too quickly. "Mami hasn't spoken to Coach Willis yet," he says.

Bernardo just shrugs. "You'll see."

○ ○ ○

The snoring continues — right above Carlos's head. He sits up. He rubs his eyes. How's he going to live with that noise? Now it kind of sounds like an animal's low growl with something choppy at the end. There's a little bit of smacking, too. Carlos waits. He knows it's not

going to stop. How can Bernardo sleep through his own snoring?

After fifteen minutes of staring at the bottom of the upper bunk, fifteen minutes of waiting for it to stop, Carlos reaches under his bed for his hockey stick. He jams the underside of the bunk, hard.

It takes a couple of jabs before Bernardo sits up. "What, what? What's going on?"

"You're snoring!"

"What?"

"You're snoring and waking me up!"

Bernardo drops his head over the edge of the bunk. "No, I'm not. I don't snore."

"Yes, you do!"

"I don't see how that's keeping you awake."

"It's *loud!*"

"Then just close your ears."

Carlos jumps out of bed and stomps to the bathroom, not caring if he wakes up the rest of the family. He grabs some toilet paper, pulls it apart, then balls up each half and stuffs it into his ears. He climbs back in bed and lies there for a moment, listening. Quiet . . . it seems at first, but then the snoring gets through the tissue. It's muffled, but still there. He stares at the underside of the top bunk. Bernardo's back to sleep. How can that be? How long is Carlos going to have to put up with him?

Seven
The Care and Feeding of Geckos

The next thing Carlos knows, Bernardo is shaking him awake and saying, "Let me feed the geckos."

It's morning. Carlos covers his eyes. "Let me wake up." He yawns.

"Come on, come on!"

Carlos pulls himself up and climbs slowly out of bed. He moves to the terrarium and stands there a moment, still waking up. Bernardo bends down to look through the glass. "Let me hold one."

"I have to give you the rules first."

"Okay, give me the rules, then."

"First, I need to tell you about geckos."

Bernardo seems suddenly bored. He looks as if he just wants to get his hand into the terrarium.

"First of all," Carlos says, "you don't play with geckos more than thirty minutes a day, and that's mainly just holding them."

Bernardo says, "Yeah, yeah . . . okay."

Carlos studies him for a few seconds. "We'll take turns feeding them. I always feed them in the morning, so you can watch me."

"Just show me how it's done," Bernardo says.

"I'm going to tell you about the geckos and the ants. And you better listen." This is going to be hard — keeping Bernardo from traumatizing his geckos or causing tunnel collapse in his ant farm.

"I'm going to start with the ant farm because it's the most . . . Well, things can happen."

"Like what?" Bernardo asks.

"Well, see all those tunnels they've made?"

Bernardo practically drools as he peers through the glass.

"They go to a lot of trouble to make them. That's why even Issy is careful when she's near the ant farm table. If this table is jiggled, you can collapse their tunnels. And they'll get buried."

"How long do they live, anyway?"

"Why?"

"Just wondering how long an ant lives."

Carlos looks at Bernardo suspiciously. The question bothers him.

"Well, that's the thing. They don't live all that long." He points out a small section of the farm near the surface. "See this here?"

Bernardo lowers himself some more, but then wobbles a little on his feet. Carlos yanks him back by his shirt collar.

"Hey!"

"I said you have to be careful around the farm!"

"I'm being careful!" Bernardo straightens.

"I was going to say, that little section is like their graveyard. It's called a midden. They carry the dead ants to it."

"An ant graveyard?" Bernardo's eyes widen. He looks back at the geckos. "Do the geckos have a graveyard?"

"No. They live longer. Pay attention."

Bernardo stares into Carlos's eyes to show he's

paying attention, but an expression crosses over his face that makes Carlos feel a little uneasy.

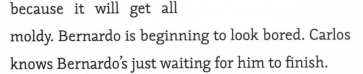

Carlos explains how the ants in the farm are western harvester ants, and they eat just about anything, but a little bit of cracker crumbs and some drops of water dripped onto the sand will do. Also, whatever they don't eat has to be taken out of the farm because it will get all moldy. Bernardo is beginning to look bored. Carlos knows Bernardo's just waiting for him to finish.

"Can I feed 'em too?"

"We'll get to that. If I think you can be careful, I'll let you feed them in a minute. Now, here are the gecko rules, so listen carefully."

"Gecko rules."

"Here's what you need to know."

Bernardo waits.

All Carlos can think is, *Can I trust this guy?*

"What are the rules?"

"Okay, first, they're leopard geckos . . ."

"That's why they have the spots."

"Right. And two are female," he reminds Bernardo.

"Girl geckos?"

"Yes," Carlos says. "'Cause males would fight each other. So you can't have two males."

Bernardo's eyes widen. "Why do they fight?"

"'Cause they both want to be the boss. It's the same with dogs."

"How do you know so much?"

"I want to be a zoologist and work with animals. Or, I want to be an entomologist — someone who studies insects and learns things and maybe works for a lab or something. I've been looking stuff up."

Carlos pulls out the bottom dresser drawer and removes a towel covering a plastic container of live crickets. The container has air holes so the crickets can breathe. Their very muffled chirping gets louder. "You mustn't overfeed geckos," he says. "Crickets are the best food, vitamin-wise. We get these at the pet store. And the crickets have to be fed too. Otherwise they eat their own poop."

Bernardo's eyes widen. "What!" He looks at the crickets in the container.

"Yeah, that's the way I felt when I first heard that. So I feed the crickets stuff like a little bit of carrots or orange. Now, you don't want to give the geckos too many crickets, 'cause they won't eat them all, and then you'll have crickets that the geckos can't finish. Then you'll be hearing them chirping all night long."

Carlos sees a little smile cross Bernardo's face.

"What's so funny?"

"Nothing."

Carlos goes on. "And — listen good — don't let any crickets get away, because that happened once and we kept hearing the chirping but we couldn't find it and . . . You just don't want that to happen."

"Okay," Bernardo says. "Can I feed the geckos now?"

Carlos is still reluctant, but he gives in and hands Bernardo the container. "Keep the lid on and listen." He instructs Bernardo to open the container inside the terrarium and carefully, *carefully,* pour just a few crickets in. Unless he wants to use his hand.

Bernardo nods quickly and reaches for the container. Carlos jerks it back. "You remember what I said, right?"

"Yeah, yeah," Bernardo says.

Carlos hands him the plastic container, slowly.

Bernardo follows Carlos's instructions. He reaches into the terrarium and shakes out three crickets. Darla notices them first. Gizmo is in the cave, and Peaches is at the far end of the terrarium. Darla freezes and stares at the cricket. The cricket seems to freeze as well.

"Watch this," Carlos says. "She's real good at this."

Bernardo's mouth drops open.

Quickly, the gecko sticks out her tongue and laps up the cricket.

"*Whoa,*" Bernardo exclaims. He turns to Carlos, eyes wide.

"See?" Carlos says. "But sometimes the

geckos have to go after the cricket, and that gives them exercise."

He tells Bernardo he can feed the ants next. He might as well let him do both. The ants are much easier. Carlos shows Bernardo how to carefully remove the plastic top of the farm to sprinkle in a few cracker crumbs and then, using the eyedropper, place a few drops of water on the sand.

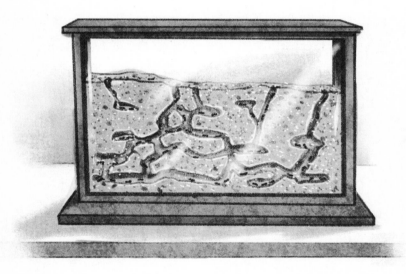

He breathes a sigh of relief when it all goes well. They watch the ants moving through their tunnels for a bit, and then Bernardo brushes the palms of his hands together like a person who's finished a great task and says, "I'm hungry. What's for breakfast?"

He turns and bounds down the stairs. Carlos takes a last look at his creatures and follows behind.

Eight
Soccer Practice

Soccer practice after school," Mami says, handing Carlos and Bernardo sack lunches. "Make sure you're standing on the school steps, pronto. Last time, we were late, and Coach Willis wasn't too pleased." She directs them to the front door. "And don't be late to school, either."

But Bernardo has a problem with lollygagging. When they pass Rick B's Junkyard, he decides to aggravate the killer guard dog by laughing and rattling the chainlink fence until the slobbering hound is rushing it, barking and snarling.

"Ha-ha," Bernardo laughs. "That dog can't do *nothin'!*" He barks back at the dog.

"Bernardo, cut it out."

"Why? He can't get me through the fence."

"Because it's not fair to the dog."

"I don't care about being fair to the dog."

They pass Global Tire and Brakes, and Bernardo sneaks into the customer waiting room to get some gumballs out of the dispenser.

Carlos calls after him that they're going to be late, but winds up saying it to Bernardo's retreating back.

Carlos decides to continue on to school by himself. If Bernardo gets lost, too bad. He's sick of Bernardo. He doesn't make his bed; he leaves his pajamas on the floor in the bathroom. And Carlos suspects that he's not really showering at night. *And* he leaves blobs of spitty toothpaste in the sink and doesn't rinse it out. How can anybody brush their teeth over that?

Last night, Carlos had brought up his complaints to Mami when Bernardo was out of earshot. "He's missing his mother," Mami explained.

"He doesn't act like it. When she calls, he gets off the phone real quick so he can get back to his video game."

"Be patient with him. He's your cousin. And family's important."

"I know. How can I forget?"

○ ○ ○

Bernardo catches up to Carlos and they reach the schoolyard just as the line-up bell rings. Bernardo gets into the line behind Carlos, chewing his gum loudly. Carlos vows to say nothing. If Bernardo gets into trouble, it'll just be too bad. No school allows gum chewing, so he won't be able to play dumb. But then Carlos thinks better of it. "You better get rid of that gum," he whispers to Bernardo. He can see Ms. Shelby-Ortiz making her way over to their line.

"What?" Bernardo says out loud.

Deja turns around and glares at him. "Shhh," she hisses. "No talking!"

Bernardo flinches. "Who's that girl?"

Carlos ignores the question. Bernardo stops the obvious chewing.

Ms. Shelby-Ortiz walks up, inspects the line, and signals for them to start for the classroom.

● ● ●

Bernardo suddenly has to make a trip to the bathroom right after school. Carlos heads to the front entrance, where Mami is probably sitting in the car, tapping the steering wheel impatiently. She's not supposed to stop right in front of the school. There's a policeman who sometimes circles the building in his patrol car at dismissal time, just so he can tell people to move along. Well, Bernardo knows where the front steps are. Better for Carlos to get out there and let Mami be annoyed with just one of them, as opposed to them both.

Carlos is happy to see that the coast is clear out front. No policeman. Mami must be running late. Bernardo saunters up just as Mami pulls in front of the school. Is the guy never in a hurry?

Carlos climbs into the back seat next to Issy. She's strapped into her kid seat because she hasn't reached the right weight to use just the seat belt. Bernardo gets in the front. Carlos sighs nervously. He's not looking forward to practice, after last week. He couldn't do anything right. Coach Willis had them work in pairs and practice passing the ball to each other. There was so much to remember: use the base of the ankle; make sure the ankle is locked on the follow-through . . . He kept messing up and annoying his partner, this kid from another school named Barton Holmby. How many times did he have to run after the ball while Barton waited with his hands on his hips and a scowl on his face?

Then he'd actually complained to Coach Willis. "Can I get another partner?" he'd called out in front of everybody. "I'm not getting enough practice."

Carlos knows Barton is a whiny kid. Always complaining and blaming others when he makes a mistake. Always getting his mother to complain about this or that, while he stands a little ways away, watching. But still, it was embarrassing.

"Do your best," Coach Willis had called back to him.

○ ○ ○

Today at practice they're paired up and practicing dribbling and passing again. Carlos looks over at Bernardo and his partner. They seem to be doing great. He knows Coach Willis is noticing. Coach will probably be thrilled to put Big Bernardo on the team. "So what else is new?" Carlos says under his breath. It's his favorite phrase.

Next, they run the cones, and Coach Willis has to keep telling Carlos and a few other players, "Keep hunched! Don't straighten." After a while, he catches sight of Bernardo and smiles broadly. "Bernardo! Get over here."

Bernardo has a funny look on his face. He's probably wondering if he's in trouble. Did he do something wrong?

Carlos watches, trying not to be obvious. After Coach Willis and Bernardo finish conferencing, Coach starts calling kids in from the field — Carlos included.

When there are about six of them standing around, Coach Willis announces, "Bernardo here is going to work with you. He's got good technique, so do what he says."

Carlos doesn't want to work with Bernardo. He doesn't want to do what Bernardo tells him. But he keeps his mouth shut as he watches Bernardo demonstrate a dribble using both the inside and the outside of his foot.

Practice is easier when Coach Willis isn't zeroing in on their technique over and over, and bringing a player's weakness to everyone's attention. Carlos is almost relieved when Coach finally blows his whistle and calls them all over to him. He says, "Okay, count off, and we'll play a little practice game." That's the way it always goes — first the skills, and then a practice game. That's when Carlos gets to run around, mimicking the other players, looking like he's doing something. Hoping he'll get better.

Sometimes he wonders why he even plays soccer. Then he remembers it's because of Papi. He wants to please Papi. Papi is a big soccer fan, so he probably keeps hoping that one day Carlos will wake up and be really good.

○ ○ ○

When Mami picks them up, Bernardo recounts in detail all the things he noticed about the other players and how Coach Willis had him help with some of the kids who just weren't getting it.

He turns to Carlos. "You need to try harder," he

says. "It looks like you're just waiting for practice to be over." Then he launches into more talk about himself. Carlos has to put up with this the entire ride home. It even carries over to dinner. And what's worse is that Papi sits there, looking interested in what he has to say.

"So Coach Willis had you helping some of your teammates?"

"Yeah." Bernardo looks over at Carlos.

"Wow! I'm not surprised." Papi turns to Carlos. "So how did you do, Carlos?"

"Bernardo was helping Carlos, too," Issy says.

"Oh?" Papi asks.

"Yeah," Carlos admits. What more is there to say?

"Just what did he have to help you with?"

Before Carlos can answer Papi's question, Bernardo pipes up with, "Carlos was having a lot of problems with dribbling and returning the ball."

"Hmm," Papi says. "So, Carlos, that's probably what you need to focus on."

"Yeah, I guess so," Carlos says.

● ● ●

He's relieved when dinner is over and he can escape to his room to check on his creatures. Papi and Bernardo will probably find some sports thing to watch on TV. Then Bernardo can show Papi what a big sports guy he is.

Nine
Where's the Woolly Mammoth's Ear?

The next morning at school, the journal topic is "My Favorite Time of Day." Carlos stares at it for a minute. He looks over at Bernardo. He's drawing some kind of action figure from *The Return of Lizard Man* on the cover of his journal. He supposes Bernardo will eventually get started writing. Sometimes Ms. Shelby-Ortiz will call for a volunteer to read their entry. He's hoping she'll do that this time. Sometimes she'll "volunteer" a person who doesn't want to read. Bernardo is pushing his luck, thinking he can just fool around like that.

Carlos opens his journal and turns to the next clean page. He writes the day's date in the upper right-hand corner. He stares at the topic on the board, then writes it on the first line. "My Favorite Time of Day." This is an easy one for him. He already knows what his favorite time of day is. It's that time when he first walks into his room after school — before Mami starts nagging him about his homework or some chore — and he looks around and thinks, *All this is mine.* When he gets his butterfly habitat, he will have the most interesting room in the world.

He likes to see what the geckos have been up to — or imagine what they've been up to in the gecko world, doing gecko things that happen just between geckos. He likes to get his snack, sneak it into his room if possible, then sit in the middle of his bed and eat it while looking down on his domain.

"Ms. Shelby-Ortiz," Calvin calls out. He's coming back from the pencil sharpener and has stopped next to the class puzzle table. Ms. Shelby-Ortiz looks up from some papers she's correcting at her desk.

"What is it, Calvin?"

"We're almost finished with the *Extinct Species* jigsaw puzzle."

"I noticed, but, Calvin, did you really need to disturb the class, calling out like that?"

Calvin returns to his seat, blowing on the sharpened pencil lead.

Carlos has filled half a journal page and still has so much more to write about his room. But before he knows it, Ms. Shelby-Ortiz is telling the class to put their pencils down. Then she says the words he's hoping to hear.

"Any volunteers who'd like to share their journal entry?"

Carlos's hand flies up. He really wants to share his entry. Unfortunately, Ms. Shelby-Ortiz is looking the other way, toward Sheila Sharpe, who's waving her hand as well. Sheila Sharpe is really shy and almost never speaks up. Ms. Shelby-Ortiz picks her instead of Carlos. She is probably trying to encourage Sheila to be more outgoing.

Carlos thinks that Bernardo should be happy Ms. Shelby-Ortiz didn't "volunteer" him. So far, the only thing he's written on his journal page is the date and one sentence.

Sheila stands up next to her desk and begins to read out loud:

"My favorite time of day is when I get home from school. My mom usually has a nice snack waiting for me, and after I finish that, my mom lets me relax before I have to do my homework. I like to go into my bedroom. That's where all my stuffed animals are. I like to play with them for a while and arrange them on my bed and look at them. My bedroom is pink and gray. I have a pink canopy bed and pink and gray curtains . . ."

Carlos stops paying attention. It's so boring. If he had been able to read his journal entry, everyone would have been really interested. He'd have gotten in some really interesting information about his geckos and his ant farm.

Stuffed animals? What does a stuffed animal do? Nothing. It just sits there where you put it last. Sits there and does nothing, with a stupid look on its face. He sighs. Calvin Vickers yawns loudly, and Ms.

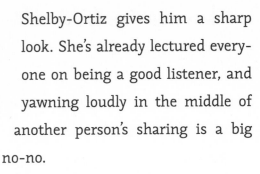

Shelby-Ortiz gives him a sharp look. She's already lectured everyone on being a good listener, and yawning loudly in the middle of another person's sharing is a big no-no.

Carlos hopes that maybe Ms. Shelby-Ortiz plans to call on someone else when Sheila Sharpe finally concludes. He checks the clock. There's still reading in pairs to do.

"And that's my favorite time of day," Sheila finally says.

Yes! Carlos thinks, and shoots his hand up. He jiggles it to draw his teacher's attention toward him. He looks around. What? Gavin's got his hand up? Now Ms. Shelby-Ortiz is looking back and forth between the two of them. *Me, me!* he thinks, and waits for Ms. Shelby-Ortiz to see the pleading in his eyes.

But her eyes go up to the clock over the whiteboard. "It looks like we need to move on. Class, get into your pairs for reading. Oh, and Carlos, remember you're with Bernardo."

Great. And he doesn't even get the pleasure of standing up and moving to a different location. All he has to do is open his book to where they left off and wait for Bernardo to dig around in his desk in search of his own book.

Bernardo finds it eventually, pulls it out, and looks at Carlos. "What page?" he asks.

Carlos tells him, then says, "I'll go first." Carlos reads the first paragraph of a story called "Monkey and Chameleon." It's actually interesting, and it gives Carlos an idea about chameleons. He wonders if it's possible to get a pet chameleon. That would be awesome. He thinks of his room. It does have space for a cage. Would a chameleon be happy in a cage? He'll have to read up on it.

He finishes the first paragraph and waits for Bernardo to pick up where he left off. There's a moment of silence while Carlos watches Bernardo stare at his paragraph. He reads the opening sentence super slowly but stops on the word *together.* Carlos tells him the word.

"I know that's *together*. I was just getting ready to say it."

Carlos waits for Bernardo to pick it up from the word *together*. Slowly, Bernardo sounds out the next sentence. He stops on *frightened,* and as soon as Carlos tells him the word, he says it quickly along with Carlos. "I already knew that word," he says.

And that's how it goes during pair-reading with Bernardo. Carlos practically reads Bernardo's paragraph for him, with Bernardo telling him over and over that he was just getting ready to say the word on his own. Carlos is relieved when Ms. Shelby-Ortiz says it's time to finish up and get ready for recess. Today they're playing basketball.

Carlos and Bernardo's table is the last to be dismissed. Gavin and Richard stand at the door, waiting for Carlos. Ms. Shelby-Ortiz finally calls Table Two, and once everyone is out of the classroom, she heads off to the teachers' lounge. Just as Carlos and Bernardo reach the doors leading out to the yard, Bernardo says, "Wait. I forgot my snack."

"You can have some of mine," Carlos says. He

really wants all the graham crackers for himself, but he guesses he can share.

"No, no . . . I want my own. I'll be back."

Room Ten's students have moved to the basketball court today, and it's Bernardo and Rosario's turn to be that day's team captains. Carlos knows it's going to end up boys against girls.

"So where's Bernardo?" Gavin asks when he sees that Bernardo hasn't made it to the court yet.

Carlos glances at the school building. "I don't know. He went back to get his snack. He's coming."

"What's he going to do with a snack? You can't have a snack on the court while you're playing basketball," Gavin says.

"Knowing Bernardo, he'll figure out a way."

"He's just going to get in trouble. Let's choose someone else to be captain."

Carlos looks toward the door again just as Bernardo's exiting. "Here he comes."

● ● ●

Somehow, Bernardo manages to eat a whole package of cheese crackers and play basketball at the same

time. Just as the bell signaling the end of recess rings, he stuffs the plastic wrapper in his pants pocket. He must have been right about being good at all sports, because he outshines everyone else on the court. He dominates the game so much that some kids just hang back when he's dribbling the ball. Emilio tries to steal it at one point, and Bernardo elbows him out of the way.

"Not fair!" Emilio cries. "You can't do that! That's a foul. I should get a free throw!"

Bernardo just carries on as if he doesn't even hear. He takes his shot. The ball bounces off the backboard and drops through the basket. Emilio stomps off the court.

One thing Carlos notices about Bernardo: he usually manages to get his way. At the lunch table later as Carlos and Bernardo unpack their sack lunches — that Mami makes at night and puts in the refrigerator — Bernardo pulls out a Toaster Tart, already toasted. Carlos has the usual three cookies for dessert. Bernardo has three cookies as well.

"Hey," Carlos says. "Where'd you get that?"

"What?"

"That Toaster Tart. My mom never puts those in our lunch. That's for after school — for a snack."

"I got it out of the cabinet and I toasted it and put it in my lunch — last night."

Carlos remembers Bernardo getting up from bed to get a drink of water. He didn't know Bernardo was going to go scavenging for extra food.

"You have to ask," Carlos says. "You can't just take what you want and put it in your lunch."

Bernardo barely manages a shrug before he takes a big bite out of the tart.

Bulldozer. That's the word that comes to Carlos's mind. Bernardo is like a bulldozer. Moving people — and rules — out of the way. He just does what he wants. And the bad thing is, he's going to be there in Carlos's life *for a while.*

● ● ●

Carlos is hurrying through his math classwork so he can get to the puzzle table. He looks around. Mostly everyone is working diligently. Even Bernardo is hunched over his worksheet. Before Carlos can get through the last problem — a word problem for which he must show his work — two hands go up. Nikki's, then Erik's. Ms. Shelby-Ortiz calls on Nikki.

"Ms. Shelby-Ortiz, I'm finished with my math. Can I . . ."

"*May* I," Ms. Shelby-Ortiz corrects her.

"May I go to the puzzle table?"

Erik's hand is waving back and forth.

"You're finished too, Erik?"

"Yes."

"Okay, you may both go ahead."

Their chairs scrape in unison across the linoleum floor as they scramble to get to the puzzle table in the corner of the classroom next to the class library. Carlos finishes the last problem, sighs, and takes out his book and stares at the page where he left off. During "free time" only two students are allowed at the puzzle table. Otherwise it can get too noisy. After a while, he glances up to see Nikki and Erik eagerly searching through the last pieces.

"This goes here," Nikki says in a loud whisper. "And this goes here."

Soon they are looking at the floor around the table. "Ms. Shelby-Ortiz, there are some pieces missing," Erik says.

Everyone looks up. A few frown.

"Did you look around the table and on the floor?"

"We looked, Ms. Shelby-Ortiz," Nikki says. "They're gone."

Rosario makes a sound of alarm. "Oh, no! What if we can't find them and then our puzzle can't be finished and then Ms. Shelby-Ortiz can't put the special glue on and then we can't hang it up for everyone to see?" She's gotten the attention of the whole class. People have put down their SSR books. Others have looked up from their math.

Antonia raises her hand and waits to be recognized. When Ms. Shelby-Ortiz nods at her, she says, "Ms. Shelby-Ortiz, if we never find the pieces, then we can just trace the spaces on cardboard and then color it and then put them in place. We can finish it that way."

There's a chorus of "Yeah, yeah, we can do that!"

That's when Carlos notices something. Bernardo, who'd been working on some kind of doodling in the upper corner of his worksheet, now looks up, with pencil poised, at Antonia. His brow furrows a tiny bit. Everyone else seems happy with the solution, but his face is blank. That's when Carlos knows Bernardo took the pieces — when he supposedly went back for his snack. His mother has explained that when people feel bad about things, they can sometimes act out. Bernardo must want the class to feel bad — like he does. Bernardo took the pieces, and Carlos is going to prove it. It's not right for Bernardo to try to make the class feel bad.

Carlos sneaks glances at Bernardo on the way home as he tells Mami how he scored most of the points in the basketball game at morning recess and lunch recess. How his team just *creamed* the other team. How now everyone wants him on their team — because he's good in every sport.

Mami has her mind on something else. Carlos can tell, because she's doing that *Uh-huh . . . Oh, really? . . . Oh, wow . . .* thing she does when she's only pretending to listen. While Bernardo is yapping, Carlos is planning. The puzzle pieces have to be on Bernardo or in his book bag. He can search the book bag when

Bernardo leaves it at the bottom of the staircase and goes into the kitchen for his snack.

But what if the pieces are in his pants pockets? *Hmm,* Carlos thinks. He won't be able to check the pants until Bernardo goes to the bathroom to take his fake shower.

○ ○ ○

"Wash your hands before you get anything to eat," Mami says as she runs to answer the ringing telephone in the den. It's probably Tía Lupe. Carlos and Bernardo both wash their hands at the kitchen sink using dishwashing liquid. Bernardo pours himself a glass of milk, and Carlos gets down the chocolate chip cookies from the cabinet.

"Be right back," he says. "I have to do something."

Bernardo hardly pays attention. He's busy opening the package of cookies.

○ ○ ○

Carlos hurries up the stairs with both book bags. That way, Bernardo will think Carlos's mother told him to clear the stairs before someone trips over them.

He hurries into his room and closes the door behind him, putting his back to it. He checks the zippered outside pocket of Bernardo's backpack. He rummages around among pencil shavings and markers and bits of papers and a sticky piece of peppermint without the wrapper. No puzzle pieces. Carlos pulls his hand out and wipes it on his jeans to no avail. Yuck.

He's unzipped the main compartment and is just beginning to search around among the three-ring binder and loose-leaf paper and something that feels like one of his own action figures when he hears Bernardo's footsteps on the stairs. He'd know that heavy clomping sound anywhere.

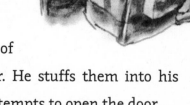

With his back still to the door, Carlos sticks his head nearly inside the backpack and shakes it. The steps grow closer. Then he sees them — three shiny pieces of the woolly mammoth's ear. He stuffs them into his pocket, just as Bernardo attempts to open the door.

"Hey, let me in," he says.

Carlos zips up the main compartment and tosses

the backpack onto the lower bunk next to his. He moves away from the door and gets on his hands and knees.

Bernardo steps into the room and gives Carlos a puzzled look. "What are you up to?"

"I dropped a marker, and it rolled behind the dresser." That seems reasonable, since the dresser is right beside the door. Looking behind the dresser would cause the door to be blocked.

Bernardo looks over at his backpack on the lower bunk. He looks back at Carlos. "Oh."

Ten
Storm Warning

Why is it that when you're dreading something, it comes super-quick? That's the way Carlos feels about soccer these days. He's been dreading Saturday's game, and here it is Friday already. Bernardo's in the bathroom singing some song that Carlos doesn't recognize at the top of his lungs.

He thinks about the puzzle pieces he retrieved from Bernardo's backpack. He'd squirreled them away in his pencil box when Bernardo wasn't looking. He could show them to Mami and get his cousin in trouble. Yeah . . . Mami — and Papi, too — think Bernardo is so great, with all his athletic prowess. Wouldn't they like to know that he took the last three puzzle pieces from the thousand-piece puzzle? And just as the class was about to finish, too. Wouldn't they like to know that Ms. Shelby-Ortiz won't be able to put the special glue on the puzzle like she'd planned? And wouldn't they like to know that there nearly went Room Ten's chance to hang the thousand-piece puzzle by the classroom door so everyone in the whole school could see it when they pass by?

Yeah, sure, Antonia came up with that idea about making their own puzzle pieces out of cardboard, but what if Antonia *hadn't* come up with that idea? All those months of hard work would have just gone to waste.

For some reason, he knows he won't tell his parents. He's not sure why. It just doesn't feel as good as it should. Will he tell Ms. Shelby-Ortiz? He doesn't know. Maybe not. It almost feels like he'd be kicking Bernardo while he's down.

He realizes when he walks into the classroom that he's not going to tell Ms. Shelby-Ortiz, either. He's not even going to tell Richard and Gavin. Because then *he'll* be the one who's embarrassed about having a bozo for a cousin. What would they think, learning that Carlos's own cousin is not only a thief, but also the kind of person who'd try to ruin stuff for the rest of the class?

Carlos says nothing. He just spends the morning doing his work, pair-reading with Bernardo, and wondering what he's going to do with the puzzle pieces. Where can he put them so they can be *found*?

The class library. He can slip them among the floor cushions. But how will they have gotten there? Maybe they can be on the floor under the bookcase. Yes, there's a gap between the bottom shelf and the floor. The pieces could have fallen on the floor and been kicked under the shelf. That's believable.

He looks around. Everyone is quietly doing their work. He takes out his pencil box, opens it, and plucks out the puzzle pieces. He slips them into his pocket, raises his other hand and waits to be recognized. He waves it around. It gets Rosario's attention. She looks over at him. Finally, Ms. Shelby-Ortiz glances up and catches sight of his hand. "Yes, Carlos."

"Can I . . . I mean, *may* I sharpen my pencil?"

Ms. Shelby-Ortiz nods.

She gives you three times to sharpen your pencil in one day. If you break the lead after that, you have to do your work with a fat kindergarten pencil — because you're not yet ready for a regular pencil. No one wants to spend the rest of the afternoon writing with a kindergarten pencil. It's embarrassing.

Carlos fingers the puzzle pieces in his pocket. He looks around, sharpens his pencil, then blows on the lead. Everyone is busy. He drops the puzzle pieces, then kicks them under the bookcase. He returns to his seat, wondering who is going to discover them. At one point while he works on his math assignment, he looks over at Bernardo, who is doodling on his workbook page. It looks like he's completed only the top row of problems. He should be nearly finished. He's not using his time wisely. That's what Ms. Shelby-Ortiz always says when she catches someone doing everything *but* completing their assignments.

Ms. Shelby-Ortiz is busy posting student work on the *Good Job!* bulletin board. They'd had to write a letter to a classmate about a place they've been to — interesting or boring. They had to remember to include supporting details after each topic sentence.

They'd pulled one another's names out of a box

without looking. Carlos had gotten Ralph's name, and Rosario had gotten his. He wrote about Zooland. There were so many interesting things to write about, he almost couldn't stop. He never knew giraffes can use their necks as a weapon in combat bouts or that the closest relative to a hippopotamus is a whale. Rosario wrote about visiting her great-aunt at a senior living facility. The only thing she'd liked were the free doughnuts in the lobby.

Antonia raises her hand.

"Yes, Antonia?" Ms. Shelby-Ortiz says.

"May I get a new book to read? I've finished this one."

Most of the class will choose the puzzle table when they finish their work early and have free time. Antonia usually chooses reading for pleasure.

"Yes, go ahead," Ms. Shelby-Ortiz says.

Carlos can't help checking Antonia every few moments as she looks for her next book. When she squats to search the bottom shelf, he holds his breath. Carlos's view of her is blocked by the bookcase. She's out of sight for what seems like minutes as she squats behind the shelf. He looks at his next problem. It's a multiplication problem with a three-digit multiplier. He begins to tackle it. But then he finally hears what he's been waiting for. "Ms. Shelby-Ortiz . . . Look what I found!"

Everyone looks up as Antonia makes her way over to the teacher with her hand extended.

"Oh, great!" Ms. Shelby-Ortiz exclaims. "Class, Antonia found the missing puzzle pieces!"

Bernardo jerks his head up from his math work. His mouth drops open a little, and he looks around the classroom, as if he's searching for an explanation.

"Can I put them in the puzzle?" Antonia asks.

Nikki throws her hand up and waves it around. Ms. Shelby-Ortiz nods at her. "But we were the ones — me and Erik were the ones who were going to finish the puzzle yesterday! We were just about to do it!"

Of course their smart teacher comes up with the perfect solution. Since there are three pieces, she hands one each to Erik, Nikki, and Antonia. "Antonia, you may put your piece in the puzzle now. Erik and Nikki, when you finish your math, you may put yours in."

A few minutes later, Nikki is the person to place the final piece in the thousand-piece puzzle. Carlos thinks she slowed down on purpose just so she could be the one to complete it. It would be like her to do something like that. She brushes her palms together and looks around as the whole class cheers. Ms. Shelby-Ortiz raises her hand to quiet them and Carlos checks Bernardo. He has his mouth poked out. He doesn't look happy. Not at all.

There are dark clouds in the sky by the time school is over. They look heavy with rain. There might be a storm coming. A big storm. As he and Bernardo walk to Mami's car, Carlos looks up and his heart races with excitement. A big storm with lots of thunder and lightning — a storm that lasts through the night and into the morning and maybe a little bit into the after- noon — could mean a canceled soccer game! He smiles as he climbs into the back seat of the car, next to Issy in her tiara.

"What's so funny?" Issy asks.

"Oh . . . nothing."

A storm with plenty of thunder and lightning would definitely mean a cancellation of the game. Everyone knows the worst place you can be during a thunderstorm is in the middle of an open field. He checks the low-lying clouds through the car's front window. They look very promising.

Of course, there's also the possibility he might not get into the game for long. With Bernardo on the team, they'll have more than eleven players. Someone will have to sit out at least part of the game and then rotate in just for a show of allowing every player a chance to play. Carlos suspects Coach Willis will do that — make sure everyone gets a chance.

Carlos looks over at Bernardo. He wonders what he's thinking. He must know that Carlos went into his backpack and found the puzzle pieces. He wonders if Bernardo is even going to say anything about it. He wonders if Big Bernardo, who knows how to punch a person for no good reason, will be mad.

● ● ●

If Bernardo's mad, he doesn't show it. At dinner, he and Papi talk about soccer. Then they switch to basketball and whether this one famous player is going to be traded to this other team. Issy whines about having to eat all of her *empanadas* because they're not the fruit kind, and Mami talks about snacks for the next day's soccer game.

Carlos looks out the window. Those same clouds are just sitting there. Doing nothing. Just sitting there, dark and gloomy, but producing *nothing*.

"Mami," he ventures.

"What, *mi hijo*?"

"You think it's going to rain?"

She looks out the window. "Mmm . . . Maybe."

"And if it rains, the game will be canceled. Right?"

"I guess." She smiles at him. "Don't worry. I don't smell rain in the air. It'll probably just pass us by."

● ● ●

Mami must be right. First thing Carlos does when he gets up the next morning is run to the window. No rain. There's a little wind and it's still overcast, but *nada* — nothing. He listens for the sounds of his mother in the kitchen preparing breakfast. He only hears the shower running. It's Mami. He knows his father is still sleeping because Mami always gets up before Papi. Then she has to shake him and shake him, go brush her teeth, and come back and shake him some more. He glances at the top bunk. Bernardo is still asleep too, on his back with his mouth open.

Carlos slips on his soccer uniform and tiptoes downstairs and out the kitchen door. He stands in the middle of the backyard and looks up at the sky. Those same stupid, useless clouds. He takes in a big breath. Does he smell rain? He can't tell. It just smells like regular air with nothing special about it.

He goes back inside and into the kitchen. What he needs is a Toaster Tart to make him feel better. He knows he's not supposed to eat Toaster Tarts for breakfast, but he's only going to eat it this one time, just to give him strength, or comfort . . . or both.

He opens the cabinet where they're kept and reaches for the box. It feels kind of light. He peers inside. *Empty!* He can't believe it. That dumb Bernardo ate the last Toaster Tart and put the empty box back. Who does that? Who eats the last of something and puts the container back on the shelf? How would Mami even know she needed to buy more with the box sitting up there in the cabinet?

● ● ●

Later, it's all he can do to keep from glaring at Bernardo while he's eating his oatmeal. Bernardo and Papi are strategizing about the upcoming game. "Remember," Papi tells him, "it's okay to retreat a little if it means getting in a better position to make the goal. Take your time. Look for openings."

Bernardo just nods as he slathers grape jelly on his toast. It's a wonder he leaves some for the rest of them. Mami chatters on and on about what she's putting in the cooler to take to the game; Issy, in her tiara, is talking about one day being old enough to play soccer herself. Papi's teasing Issy and laughing. Everyone is in a good mood. Carlos feels sick to his stomach.

● ● ●

It's just his luck that the twelfth team member, a kid named Ellis Warrington, is sick with the flu. Carlos hears Coach Willis tell Barton Holmby's mother that no one will be on the bench today and he's really counting on Barton to do his part.

Carlos knows that Coach Willis is just saying that to Barton's mother so she won't start nagging him about putting Barton in the game. Carlos may be bad, but he's not as bad as Barton. Nobody is as bad as Barton. In Carlos's opinion.

○ ○ ○

The game starts off okay. The referee places the ball in the center of the field and blows her whistle. Everyone but Carlos is off and running. Well, he's running, but he's doing his running up the field and down the field in his usual staying-away-from-the-ball fashion, unless it comes and practically stops at his feet. He knows he's disappointing Papi by not playing more aggressively, but he's gotten kicked in the shin a few too many times. The players don't wear shin guards, because Coach Willis says the team is not at that level yet. Carlos doesn't know what "at that level yet" means.

Suddenly Bernardo breaks away with the ball, kicking it toward the goal, far ahead of the other players. Carlos can hear Papi cheering him on. Feeling safe, Carlos follows with his teammates. Bernardo kicks a nice low shot into the goal, and though the goalie makes a dive for it, he misses. Parents cheer and Papi thrusts his fist in the air. The score is now one to zero, thanks to Bernardo.

The other team gets the ball, and Carlos runs up and down the field again. Then the ball is kicked right to him! Out of nowhere, a player from the other team — a girl! — steals it away and charges toward the goal. But not for long. Brian Weaver from his team gets the ball back, but he kicks too soon and it goes out of bounds behind the goal. The girl, Charlotte something (Carlos can't remember her name), gets to do a corner kick, and sends it sailing right to her team's best player, who kicks it smoothly into the goal. Cheers go up from the parents on the other side of the field. The score is one to one.

● ● ●

It's still one to one right up until the last seven minutes of the second half of the game. Carlos continues to let his teammates make most of the effort. Once, he gets to take a corner kick; he puts up his hand to signal he's about to kick the ball toward his teammates.

In this way he's able to appear important—like a real participant.

He glances over at Mami. She's sipping coffee from her thermos. Papi is eating chips out of a bag, and Issy is drinking from a juice box.

Carlos likes the time after the game is over the best. Then they have a picnic on a blanket, with sandwiches and cold drinks. Papi uses that time to give Carlos pointers like planning his free kicks or throw-ins better, or searching out and passing to the player who's in a good position. Papi must not know how hard that is to do with everyone moving around. Then he'll complain about some stuff the referee missed. Then he'll muse about taking over the task of refereeing himself. "I know I could do a better job," he always says.

Carlos is thinking about the picnic lunch and how the game is almost over when he discovers himself near the goal. Somehow the ball is suddenly skittering right at him — a straight shot, only an inch or two above the ground. He's the only one on his team in a position to stop it.

He finds himself helplessly mesmerized by its speed and accuracy. He just needs to stick out his foot or kick it away or do something. He decides to try for a kick.

Wrong choice.

If he had just stuck his foot out, it would have deflected the ball and sent it off in another direction. But no. He wanted some of Bernardo's glory. He decided to kick the ball away from the goal instead. But his foot slips over the top of the ball and does nothing to stop it. It makes its way right into the side of the net before the goalie can get to it.

A wild cheer goes up from the parents and family members on the visitors' side of the field. It sounds as if it's coming from underwater — slow and wobbly. Carlos looks over at Papi. Papi has his head in his hands. Then Papi is raking his fingers through his hair. Carlos feels nauseated again. Mami has this awful look of sadness mixed with pity on her face, and Issy is without expression. She doesn't know what's

going on, anyway. *She doesn't even count when it comes to opinions,* Carlos thinks as the referee blows the whistle signaling the end of the game.

The other team runs cheering toward the player who scored the goal. Several grab him in a bear hug. Carlos's teammates just walk glumly off the field. A few look over at him with stony expressions of disappointment and accusation. Has he ever felt so low?

Instead of their picnic being festive, it's just something to get over with. Bernardo's face is fixed in a scowl that he seems determined to keep up. The loss doesn't affect his appetite, however. He eats two of Mami's chicken salad sandwiches, a bag of chips, and eight (Carlos counted them) medium-size chocolate chip cookies, and drinks two bottles of fruit punch.

The ride home is silent. Carlos knows Papi wants to talk about the game but Mami probably gave him instructions not to. Especially while he's angry. He might say something that he'll want to take back later. Mami doesn't believe that saying "sticks and stones may break my bones, but words can never hurt me." She thinks that's ridiculous. You can heal from broken bones. But words can break a heart that won't ever fully heal.

So Papi says nothing. But the silence is worse.

Bernardo, probably taking a cue from Papi, also says nothing. But he keeps sighing loudly, making his feelings known. Issy points her juice box toward Carlos and with sad eyes says, "You can have my juice box, Carlos. I saved you some." She must sense that he feels bad. He wants to give her a hug for being the one person he has not disappointed.

Eleven
What's That Noise?

Carlos has been in the doghouse before, so he recognizes the signs. For the next few days, it's as if the game never happened. It's like a taboo subject that everyone is determined not to mention. Mami is back to gossiping with Tía Lupe. Issy is now casting her stuffed animals as subjects to her throne. He can hear her in her room, bossing them around and making them wait on her. Which is ridiculous, because she actually winds up waiting on herself.

But even though the game is not mentioned, Carlos can't shake the guilt of disappointing Papi. He knows Mami's not really all that concerned, nor is Issy. And who cares what Bernardo is thinking? But Papi . . . that's another story.

Carlos decides to put the game out of his mind. But on Monday morning, just as Carlos is getting ready to feed his geckos, Bernardo decides to give him some "advice."

"Sorry, Carlos, but you're just not that good of a player. Next time, just stop the ball, okay?"

Luckily, Mami calls up the stairs just then to tell Carlos he forgot to drag the cans to the curb and she thinks she hears the trash truck on the next block. Soon he'll have to hear Mami's usual lecture about responsibilities and how it's important to develop a work ethic when you're young and how everybody in a family should be willing to pitch in and . . . It can go on and on.

He hurries downstairs and out the kitchen door, grabs hold of the recycling bin, and drags it to the curb just as the blue truck for recyclables is pulling up in front of the house next door.

He breathes a sigh of relief. The green truck and the trash truck come later on in the morning.

He pulls the remaining bins to the curb, brushes his palms together, and strolls back to the house. But a funny feeling comes over him just as he reaches the bottom of the staircase.

"Did you make it in time?" Mami calls out.

"Yes, Mami," Carlos says as he dashes up the stairs to his room.

Bernardo is standing next to the terrarium with the container of crickets in his hand. "I already fed them," he says, indicating the geckos. For some reason, he only briefly looks Carlos in the eye.

"What's wrong?" Carlos asks.

"Nothing." Bernardo shifts from one foot to the other.

Carlos looks in the terrarium. Nothing seems out of the ordinary. Darla is in her cave. Peaches is next to it, and Gizmo is up on top, asleep. All appears fine. Carlos breathes a sigh of relief. Almost. He still feels that there's something not quite *right*.

The school day is uneventful. On Mondays, they get their spelling tests from the week before and the new words for the upcoming test. Ms. Shelby-Ortiz has Deja pass them out. Carlos doesn't like it when Deja passes back the tests. She doesn't maintain a blank look on her face. If someone gets a low score, she raises her eyebrows and chuckles to herself. If someone gets one hundred, she purses her lips and raises one eyebrow. And she doesn't always remember to put the tests face-down on the desks the way Ms. Shelby-Ortiz tells them to. Ms. Shelby-Ortiz is always talking about respecting your fellow classmates and putting yourself in their shoes and keeping their privacy when passing back things like tests and reports.

Deja is making her way over to Carlos. He holds his breath. He needs a hundred. He needs to make Papi proud of him after Saturday's soccer match. He needs to make Papi see that he's going to be successful in life even if he *isn't* the best soccer player in the world.

Deja stands over him, sighs, and purses her lips. She raises one eyebrow as she places the paper face-down on his desk. He waits until she continues on to the next table before lifting one corner of the paper. He sees a one. He lifts a little more. He sees the two zeros and a happy face. Tears nearly come to his eyes. He did it! One more hundred, and he gets his butterfly habitat. Well, *something* is going right.

He doesn't even need to look at Bernardo's test to know what he got. Just the fact that he quickly shoved it into his desk, barely looking at it, tells Carlos he didn't do well. Carlos needs to teach Bernardo how to get himself out of the Knucklehead Club.

That afternoon, Bernardo and Papi go out in the back-yard to do drills. Bernardo hurried through his home-work just so he could get outside to practice. Papi is trying to show him a scissor movement used to juke a player from the other team. What? Is Bernardo Papi's new son? Just because he's a quick learner with sports? From up in his room, Carlos can hear Papi marveling over how he had to show Bernardo scissors only once and he's already doing it perfectly.

During dinner he raves over Bernardo's technique while Bernardo smiles sheepishly and Mami tries to signal to Papi with a quick shake of her head. Carlos knows what that's all about. Mami doesn't think Papi should be praising Bernardo so much after Carlos's performance at Saturday's game.

Then Issy pipes up with, "I think Carlos is good too."

Carlos has to watch Papi smile sadly and look down at his corn soup.

"Papi, I got a hundred on my spelling test today. After dinner I'll show it to you," he offers.

Papi looks up and brightens. Or pretends to. "Good, Carlos. Good job."

"You said I could get the butterfly habitat if I made five one hundreds in a row."

"Yeah, I did. And you'll get it, I promise."

Papi doesn't seem nearly as thrilled as when Bernardo did those perfect scissors.

◉ ◉ ◉

It isn't snoring that wakes up Carlos in the middle of the night this time. It's *chirping!* Somewhere, a cricket is chirping. Carlos sits straight up. Of course, Bernardo is sound asleep above him, snoring softly. What else is new?

Carlos throws off the covers, gets up, and moves to the center of his room. He listens. Soon he hears it again. Where is it coming from?

Bernardo stirs. Carlos makes his way out into the hall. A light goes on in his parents' room. *Oh, no.* Mami comes out into the hallway while slipping on her robe.

"What on earth?" She glares at Carlos. "Is that one of your crickets?"

"I didn't do it, Mami."

"Well, how did it get out?" She looks back toward her room and slowly shakes her head. "Your *papi* can sleep through anything."

Next Issy is coming out of her room, rubbing her eyes. "What's that noise, Mami?"

"One of Carlos's crickets. Go back to bed."

Issy's eyes widen. "Is it going to get me?"

"No," Mami says. "Don't worry. We're going to find it. Go back to bed."

Issy looks unsure, but she goes back to her room and closes the door behind her.

Now it's Mami and Carlos standing in the middle of the upstairs hallway listening and listening. Carlos

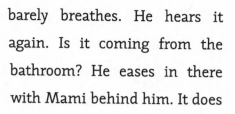

barely breathes. He hears it again. Is it coming from the bathroom? He eases in there with Mami behind him. It does sound louder. They check the floor. Nothing. Where is it? It sounds so close.

"Go check in your room again, Carlos." Mami starts down the stairs.

Carlos steps into his room and turns on the light. He bangs the door against the wall. Bernardo sits straight up. "What? What?" he says, sounding disoriented. He rubs his eyes.

"Good," Carlos says. "You're awake!"

"What's going on?"

"You let out one of the crickets!

And now it's chirping somewhere and we don't know where it is!"

"I didn't do it," Bernardo says, his eyes wide as if he's trying to make himself look as innocent as possible.

"You knew one got away. I know you did!" Carlos says in a loud whisper.

Bernardo frowns, but he doesn't say anything.

"All you can do is play soccer real good. But you snore, you don't follow the rules about feeding geckos, and you ate the last Toaster Tart and then put the box back in the cabinet. *Empty!* Plus you leave your pajamas on the bathroom floor. You spit toothpaste into the sink and don't even rinse it out!"

Bernardo just looks at Carlos. But Carlos isn't finished! "And you don't even do your best at school!" Carlos stops to think. "I about fall asleep when we do pair-reading. 'Cause I have to tell you almost every word!"

Bernardo's mouth drops open. He doesn't look mad. He looks sad. He closes his mouth and just sits there, staring down at Carlos.

"And you gave me a punch in the arm when I first met you, for no reason! I can't wait for your mother to come and take you somewhere else!"

Bernardo hangs his head. After a moment he says, "It was supposed to be like what you see athletes do. You know. They're always punching each other, but not to hurt each other. It's just something they do to be friendly."

Carlos frowns. How could Bernardo think punching someone in the arm is being friendly? Especially someone you haven't seen in ages. But Carlos believes him. It would be just like Bernardo to think that punching someone in the arm is a friendly thing to do.

"Plus you stole the last three pieces of our class's thousand-piece jigsaw puzzle! And you knew we were looking forward to hanging it on our wall so other kids could see it and wish *they* had done a thousand-piece puzzle."

"I did not," Bernardo insists.

"Bernardo — I found the pieces in your backpack!"

Bernardo doesn't say anything.

"Why, Bernardo? *Why?*"

He looks down and shrugs. "I don't know."

Carlos sighs. Now he knows how his mother feels when she asks him why he did some stupid thing and all he can say is, "I don't know."

"How come you didn't tell on me?" Bernardo finally asks. "How come you just made it so someone would find them on the floor?"

"Good question," Carlos says.

Mami tiptoes into the room then. She holds up her hand, which is softly closed over a tissue. "Found it," she says. "In the bathtub." She tiptoes to the ter-rarium, slides open the top, reaches in, and shakes the cricket out of the tissue. Carlos doesn't know why she's being so quiet. The only one asleep is Papi, and he could sleep through anything. She sighs. "Problem solved."

Bernardo lies back down. Carlos climbs into the bottom bunk. And Mami turns off the light.

Twelve
The Coming and Going Party

Bernardo is quiet the next morning. He's up before Carlos, who can hear water running in the bathroom. Carlos feels a little uneasy. Maybe he shouldn't have come down so hard on Bernardo — making him feel bad about his reading and pointing out his messiness. And all this time he's been thinking that punch was out of meanness, not out of friendliness. He thinks about this for a few moments before he realizes someone is knocking on his door. It's Issy. He can tell by the knock. "What do you want, Issy?"

"Something."

Typical five-year-old answer.

"Come in."

The door remains closed for a moment before she slowly opens it.

"What is it, Issy? Can't you see I need to get ready for school?"

She stands there silently. Her mouth turns down and begins to quiver in the corners.

"What's *wrong?*" Carlos asks. It's hard to be patient.

"I did something bad."

Carlos sighs. "What did you do?"

"I thought I could feed the geckos. I thought I could surprise you."

"What?" Carlos has a sinking feeling.

"I forgot to be careful when I shook some out of the little box thing." Issy begins to whimper. "And one got away."

"Issy, you should have told me."

"I thought you'd be mad."

Carlos does feel a jolt of anger. But he doesn't let on. "Mami found it anyway. In the bathtub," he says.

"She did?"

"Yeah. But if you do that again, Issy, I'm telling. And you will get in big trouble. You know you aren't supposed to mess with my things — especially my geckos. And my ant farm," he adds quickly. "You better not do that again."

"I won't. I promise."

● ● ●

Now Carlos feels doubly bad about blasting Bernardo. He feels bad during breakfast and on the ride to school. During morning journal time, he's tempted to write about it, but he decides to write about the cricket instead — leaving out the part about blaming Bernardo when Bernardo was innocent.

During recess, he pretends nothing happened. Bernardo pretends as well, because he doesn't even mention it. Room Ten still has the basketball court, and Ralph, who had to stay in for not doing his homework, let Bernardo take his place as team captain. Bernardo chooses Carlos for his first pick. That makes Carlos feel worse. Carlos even felt bad during pair-reading earlier each time he had to tell Bernardo a word.

He wishes he'd known that punch was meant to be friendly.

Could anything be worse than watching Bernardo just stare out the car window on the way home? *He's probably real homesick,* Carlos thinks. *He's probably wishing he were home in Texas with Tía Emilia. He's probably wishing he still had his father instead of just uncles. He's probably even wishing Papi was his father.*

Carlos needs to apologize to Bernardo. He needs to understand why Bernardo said only once that he wasn't the one who let the cricket out. No one's going to believe you if you say it only once.

Carlos looks over at his cousin, who's still looking out the window. Just as Carlos is on the verge of getting Bernardo's attention so he can tell him that he was wrong to accuse him, Mami pipes up with, "Listen. I've got a big surprise!"

"What, Mami?" Issy asks. She's wearing a macaroni necklace and bracelet that she made in kindergarten that morning. It's painted blue.

"I'll tell you when we get home."

Just then Carlos notices Issy's not wearing her tiara.

"Where's your tiara, Issy?" he asks. He knows she's not allowed to wear it in school, but she usually leaves it in the car and puts it on first thing when she gets in after school.

"I left it at home, because I'm not a queen anymore."

"Why?" Carlos asks.

"'Cause I don't want to be."

So the queen phase is over. Carlos is surprised. He forgets all about apologizing to Bernardo.

○ ○ ○

Mami sits them down at the kitchen table, her face beaming as she gets them settled with cookies and milk. She takes a seat across from them.

"Guess who's coming? Right here, on Saturday."

Bernardo is silent. Carlos tries to think of who it could be. Then it hits him. He almost feels disappointed. "Tía Emilia," he says.

Mami looks surprised and a little let down. "How did you know?" she asks.

"I just guessed."

"Her neighbor Mrs. Ruiz's son-in-law is a dentist, who lives here. He needs a new office manager, and

Mrs. Ruiz has convinced him to hire your mother, Bernardo. They even found her a place to live for now. It's small, but your mother can look for someplace bigger after she gets here." Mami's eyes shine. "Isn't it wonderful how things can just fall into place?" She looks at Bernardo, and her smile fades a little.

"Aren't you happy, Bernardo?" she asks.

"Yes. I'm happy," he says. But Carlos thinks he should sound happier.

● ● ●

There's going to be a party. A welcoming party for Tía Emilia and a going-away party for Bernardo. Everyone is coming. All the relatives. And the best thing is that they're coming with food. Carlos thinks of the sweet stuff: *empanadas* stuffed with fruit, *tamales de dulce*. There'll also be yummy chicken enchiladas and tortilla soup, *arroz con leche*, and the list goes on and on. Carlos remembers how good the Mexican dishes taste at a party. He can understand what Mami is talking about when she reminisces about the food of her childhood. Or when she and Papi disagree about who makes the best *mole*—her *tía* Hortensia or his *tía* Nelly. Whoever it is, it *isn't* Mami. She complains about her own *mole* each time she prepares it: *"I think it's too runny. Is it bland? Did I make it spicy enough? Oh, no . . . I'm beginning to cook American."*

Carlos wonders what the big deal is about *mole*. It's just this brown saucy stuff. It's all the same to him. He'd rather have spaghetti with meatballs.

● ● ●

Sure enough, the parade of food begins in the late afternoon. Mrs. Ruiz brings *arroz con pollo* and her daughter comes with a nice big pan of flan. Tía Lupe arrives with a huge plate of *empanadas* and a gallon of pink *horchata*. Her three daughters just bring themselves.

They're all Issy's age or younger, so Carlos directs them to the backyard, where Issy has set up rows of her stuffed animals in front of a chalkboard for school. Now she wants to be a teacher, so she's teaching her stuffed animals letters and sounds.

Bernardo and the uncles and two cousins, who are in college but home for the weekend, are in the living room watching a soccer match on TV. Brazil and Germany are playing. At one point, Papi tells Carlos to go to the kitchen and get more chips and salsa.

"*Salsa verde*," Papi says. "Not the red." Before Carlos can open the kitchen door, he hears Tía Lupe say, "Poor Bernardo, to have his father die when he was so young — too young to remember him. I feel so happy that he has his uncle now to pay him some attention."

His uncle... Carlos knows Tía is referring to Papi. Now he feels extra bad about all the things he said to Bernardo. He gets the chips and *salsa verde* and returns to the den, where there's a lot of whooping and hollering going on. Bernardo is joining in too. He seems happy to be a part of the group. He looks like he belongs. During halftime, Tío Raúl gets everybody outside — Papi, the cousins from college, the uncles, Bernardo — for an impromptu game of soccer just for fun, without all the rules.

Carlos decides to join in so that it's him, Bernardo, and the cousins against Papi and the uncles. Back and forth, back and forth the ball goes without anyone keeping score and with Carlos running first one way and then the other. When halftime is over, the men go back inside the house. Bernardo and Carlos stay outside.

Carlos says, "I have to tell you something, Bernardo."

Bernardo flops down on the back porch steps, and Carlos sits beside him.

"What?" Bernardo asks.

Carlos looks down. "I have to apologize." The words feel funny in his mouth. Maybe he's never said them before. He can't remember saying them. Unless it was one of those occasions when he'd done something mean to Issy and Mami said, "Apologize to your sister." Then he'd only mouthed the words. He never really meant it then, but later he'd feel bad. But this time he does mean it, right then and there.

Bernardo looks at him, waiting.

"It was Issy who let the cricket out. She told me. I shouldn't have thought it was you. And I shouldn't have gotten mad at you and said all those mean things."

Now Bernardo looks down, as if he's embarrassed. But when he brings his head up, he has a smile on his face. "You really suck at soccer. You're really bad."

"I know," Carlos says.

"You need to try harder. You can't just run up and

down the field. You have to get in there and do something."

"I know," Carlos says again, and realizes it actually makes him feel better — to have Bernardo criticizing him.

Bernardo stands up and runs to the ball. "Get up," he calls to Carlos.

Carlos obeys.

Bernardo passes the ball to him. "Use the inside of your foot and kick it back, but keep it low."

Carlos's foot slides under the ball, and the kick is too high.

"This is going to take some work," Bernardo says, but he passes it back. This time, Carlos manages to get it to Bernardo. They do that for a while, until Bernardo says, "Now use the outside of your foot."

That feels awkward — at first. But with Bernardo gently passing the ball to him, he soon gets the hang of it. Part of his "sucking at soccer" comes from not really trying all that hard. He can see that now. Maybe he should have tried harder to be Bernardo's friend, too. They didn't even go to Miller's Park or to the store for candy. But the opportunity is not lost, because Bernardo is going to be living nearby and he's still going to be in Room Ten. Carlos is still going to have his cousin.

● ● ●

The doorbell rings — right after someone has scored a goal in the game on TV and everyone inside has shouted and pumped their fists.

Bernardo runs in, with Carlos behind him, like he knows it's his mother. He arrives at the door just as Mami is opening it and folks have gathered around. There is Tía Emilia, standing on their front porch with two big pieces of luggage. The relatives, one after the other, begin to hug and welcome her as she smiles and looks around. She sees Bernardo then, and he sees her. The crowd of family members parts so mother and son can give each other a big hug.

Tía Emilia's eyes fill with tears. "Though it's only been a little while, I've missed you so much, *mi hijo*," she says.

Bernardo seems suddenly shy. "I'm glad you're here, Mami," he says finally.

Everyone goes back to whatever they were doing. Bernardo takes his mother's luggage and puts it in the hall closet out of the way. Then Tía Emilia follows Mami to the kitchen so she can visit with her sisters, and the party resumes. It seems that laughter is coming from everywhere.

● ● ●

Later, when everyone has gone home and Tía Emilia has packed up Bernardo and taken him with her —

after all the hugs and thank-yous and now-that-I'm-here-we'll-be-seeing-a-lot-of-each-others . . . After all of that, Carlos finally gets to climb up into his top bunk and survey his room. It's back to being all his, at last. Can anything be better?